Milo's friends in the dark

Created by Craig Ploetz
and Rich Koslowski

Milo Productions, Publishers
Milwaukee, Wisconsin

Milo's Friends in the Dark

Copyright © 1992 by Craig T. Ploetz and Richard K. Koslowski, Milo Productions.

Printed in the United States of America. All rights reserved.

Bound by Midwest Editions, Inc.

Printed by Litho Specialties, Inc.

ISBN# 1-882172-00-0

Library of Congress Catolog Card Number 93-187695

This book is dedicated
to the love and support
of the families.

"Milo, put out that light and get to bed."

Does the dark frighten you,
or do you like things of the stranger kind,
things that darkness make hard to find?

If you do,
then come with me.
In the dark,
there are things to see.

Down
the stairs
beneath the
floor...

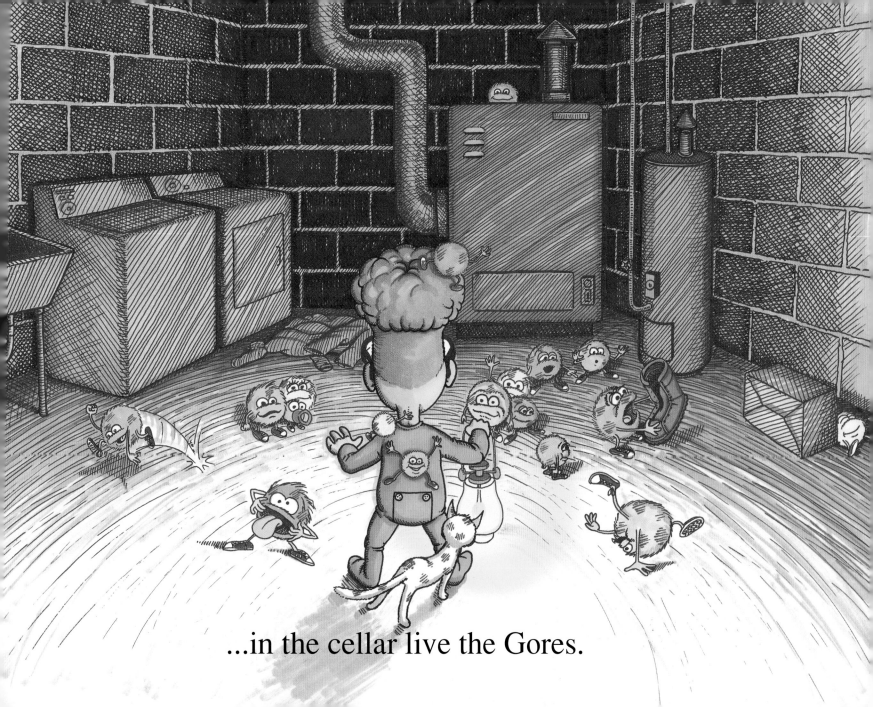

...in the cellar live the Gores.

Gores are fuzzy balls of fun
who love to roll instead of run.
Gores keep basements nice and neat
because basements have
the stuff Gores eat.

Gores eat things they find down there
like dad's old boots and balls of hair,
dampened rugs and garden hose,
Gores love lint they find on clothes.

If you should meet a Gore, ask him how does he do,
because Gores are friends we all can use.

There's
another dark place
that you should know,
it's inside your drain
where Finkies grow.
Finkies live in watery holes
like sinks and tubs and toilet bowls.

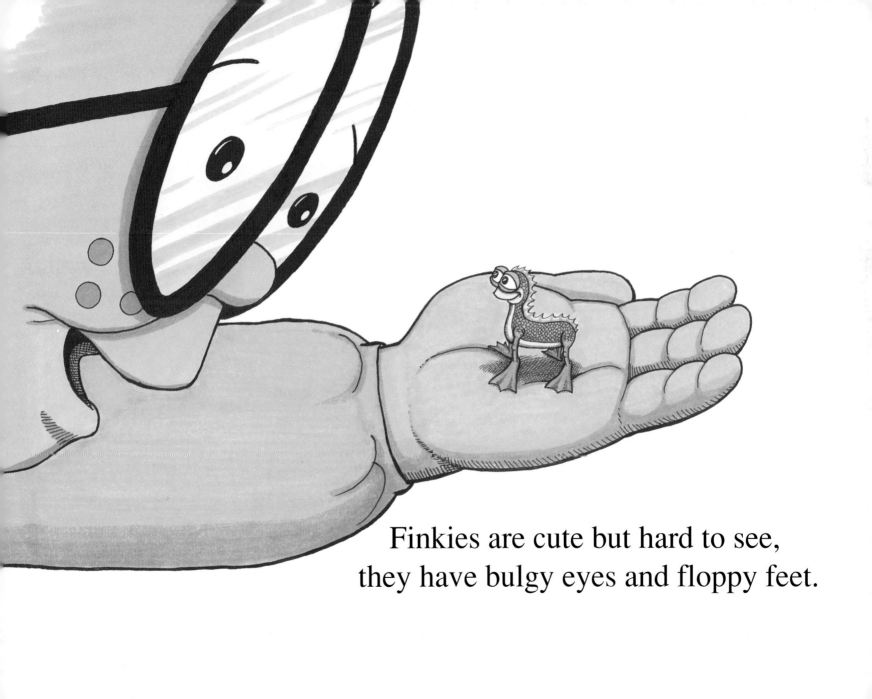

Finkies are cute but hard to see,
they have bulgy eyes and floppy feet.

Safe beneath their watery places,

Finkies stare and make silly faces.

Finkies make sure
you wash your feet,
comb your hair,
and floss your teeth.
So remember to think
next time you brush your teeth
of the friendly Finkies
inside your sink.

Come with me now to a place that creaks,
the place is the attic, the home of the Squeaks.

Squeaks have a job
which is most unique,
they plug up the holes
when your roof has leaks.

Squeaks make sounds
that sound like creaks
when they work in their boots
too tight for their feet.

Squeaks have friends
called Ceiling Trolls
that use their toes
to seal these holes.

Working together they form a team,
so you stay dry to dream your dreams.

The closet was always a spooky place, when darkness filled my closet space. Beneath my covers I used to hide, being much too scared to look inside.

But then one night
I could hide no
more.

I looked behind
the closet door.

What I found
was something to
see.
It shook up and
down and looked
like a tree.

It started to talk
this tiny tree,
he said that he too
was frightened of me.

We laughed for a while
and soon became friends.
We danced in the dark
'til my mother walked in.

"Milo", she said,
"get back to bed.
It's getting too late
you should be asleep."

I kissed her good night,
and good night to the tree.

There's one last thing that must be said,
of the darkness place beneath your bed.
When Shadows fall late at night,
the Shadows beneath your bed have life.

Now what could be alive down there,
your socks, your shoes, a fallen bear?
It's none of these so don't be scared,
   it's only Shadows that float on air.

When Shadows dance
across your room,
they clean your floor
like tiny brooms.
Sweeping away the
fears of night,
the Shadows make sure
that you sleep tight.

So put out those lights and dream your dreams, there's nothing to fear as you can see. The dark is full of friendly faces, each with a home in their night time places. You see, you're never alone they're always there to keep you company when you feel scared.

Good night,
    sweet dreams.

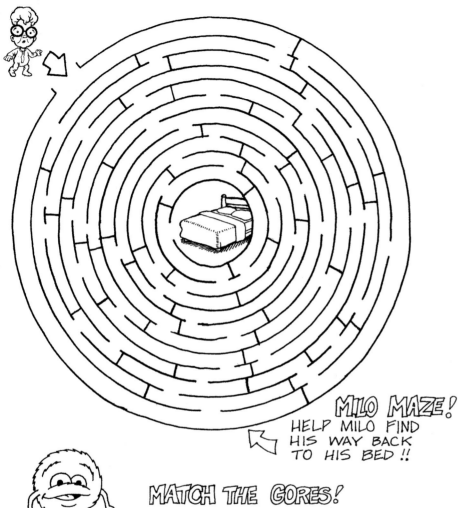

MILO MAZE!
HELP MILO FIND HIS WAY BACK TO HIS BED!!

```
R S O M M E K B F G O X F Z S
K H H I L O P B R H O I J L Q
O F O A M S A N D Y Q R L K U
S E W M D A R K E O U O E A A
L E C A I O U F F D R D G S L
O R C T R N W I I T A T Q C M
W T A N W C N K G O R P A N N
S T T O O F I N K I E S F B R
K E Q E U I I X W Z Q N R T E
I S J J U L Y R J U P O A X T
B O H Y I N Z F E I L O I L N
C L O E X S X A M I G F D N A
S C C E G S K R O L I M N A L
M G F R A S W C P L O E T Z L
F M A F R I E N D S Q P D L A
```

MILO
CEILING TROLLS
GORES
FINKIES
SQUEAKS
DARK

LANTERN
CAT
SHADOW
FRIENDS
CLOSET TREE
AFRAID

WORD SEARCH!
FIND THE WORDS ABOVE HIDDEN IN THE PUZZLE. NOW REMEMBER, THEY CAN BE BACKWARDS, FORWARD, DIAGONAL, OR UPSIDE DOWN!!

MATCH THE GORES!
◁ THIS GORE HAS A TWIN STANDING BELOW. FIND HIS EXACT MATCH!!

FOR EXTRA FUN COLOR IN THE CHARACTERS AND WORDS!